SINDHU AND JEET'S MISSING STAR MYSTERY

CHITRA SOUNDAR

ILLUSTRATED BY AMBERIN HUQ

BLOOMSBURY EDUCATION

LONDON   OXFORD   NEW YORK   NEW DELHI   SYDNEY

BLOOMSBURY EDUCATION
Bloomsbury Publishing Plc
50 Bedford Square, London, WC1B 3DP, UK
29 Earlsfort Terrace, Dublin 2, Ireland

BLOOMSBURY, BLOOMSBURY EDUCATION and the Diana logo are trademarks of
Bloomsbury Publishing Plc

First published in Great Britain in 2022 by Bloomsbury Publishing Plc

A catalogue record for this book is available from the British Library

ISBN: PB: 978-1-8019-9125-4; ePDF: 978-1-8019-9123-0; ePub: 978-1-8019-9124-7

2 4 6 8 10 9 7 5 3 1

Text design by Sarah Malley

Printed and bound in the UK by CPI Group Ltd, CR0 4YY

To find out more about our authors and books visit www.bloomsbury.com
and sign up for our newsletters

CONTENTS

The New Will   7

The Missing Star   37

A Ring Of Mystery   64

THE NEW WILL

DING-DONG!

Sindhu put down her copy of *The Handbook for Young Detectives* and sighed. That would be Jeet, the other half of Sindhu and Jeet's Detective Agency. They were both expected to attend a memorial gathering for Mrs Barker, a woman who used to live down the road.

Jeet bounded into Sindhu's room full of inappropriate enthusiasm.

"Good morning, Sindhu."

"I don't want to go," said Sindhu. "I didn't even know Mrs Barker."

"No problem," he replied. "I made a fact sheet about her for you."

Sindhu groaned. "Boring!"

"Not this one," he said. "It starts with a joke."

"*What did Mrs Barker say to the dog when she brought out her specially prepared dog food?*"

"Bone appetit!" guessed Sindhu. "I've read that one before."

"OK, fine, here's another one."

"*What do you call a detective who looks for dogs?*"

Sindhu tapped her pencil on her book. "Hmm, what?"

"Sherlock Bones," said Jeet, giggling.

Sindhu groaned. "Please just dig out the facts about Mrs Barker."

"Here we go," said Jeet and started to read the facts aloud.

1. Mrs Barker was super rich.

2. She lived in a large two-storey house at the end of the street, with big black gates. At the back, there is that legendary mindfulness garden everyone's always going on about.

3. She loved dogs. She loved all sorts of dogs. Big, small, loud, quiet, young, old, abandoned or strays.

4. Mrs Barker wrote a book called Mrs Barker's Cookbook of Dog Treats, which sold over two kazillion copies.

"Hang on a minute," said Sindhu. "Mrs Barker is very rich. That means all her money will now go to someone she loved."

"It will go to someone whether or not she loved them," said Jeet.

"I've just been reading Chapter 7 in my handbook – *Sudden Deaths and Suspicious Windfalls* – and it says in there that relatives always fight over the money left behind."

"Well, according to fact number 5, that's not a problem."

5. She had no kids. Just one nephew — Edwin.

"Right, then Edwin gets everything and there's no one who will fight him over the money," said Sindhu. "Boring!"

"Last fact," said Jeet. "The most delicious fact of all."

6. My mum is going to lay out a spread of biscuits — cream-filled ones, jam-filled ones and butter biscuits too.

"Now I get your totally inappropriate

enthusiasm," Sindhu said, with a laugh.

"Sindhu! Jeet!" Mum's voice floated up the stairs. "Time to go."

*

Inside Mrs Barker's house, a giant poster of her book cover was displayed prominently on the living room wall. People were seated on steel chairs waiting for something to happen. Sindhu and Jeet went closer to look at the poster before they settled into two seats at the back of the crowd.

"Look! My mum is bringing out the biscuits," said Jeet, pointing at his mum carrying a tray.

"I wish they would start soon,"

said Sindhu. "I don't like sitting quietly in one place."

"There's going to be music and dancing, according to my mum," said Jeet.

"What?"

"Yeah, Mrs Barker was always happy and having fun, according to my mum."

"According to your mum, when can we go home?" asked Sindhu.

"Where's your sense of mystery?" teased Jeet. "Let's play 'What-if'!"

Sindhu brightened up. She loved the game of 'What-if' that detectives played. It helped them to think about the mystery in hand.

What if Mrs Barker is not really dead? What if she is hiding and watching all of us?

What if Mrs Barker had disappeared because she drank a magic potion?

What if Mrs Barker had uncovered a treasure map in her mindfulness garden and went to find the treasure?

What if she had run away because the dogs from the shelter smelled of poo?

But not everyone was in a playful mood or as happy and fun as Mrs Barker had been. The man sitting in front of them turned around and scowled.

"Stop babbling!" he snapped.

Sindhu sunk lower in her seat as Jeet blurted out a quick sorry.

The man shot up from his chair and rushed to the front of the gathering.

"He's impatient," Sindhu said.

"I think he is the nephew, Edwin," whispered Jeet.

"There is no mystery here," said Sindhu, bored. "Rich woman dies, leaves her wealth to rude nephew. End of story. No one lives happily ever after."

"There is definitely a mystery," said Jeet. "Whether the cream-filled biscuits on the table are full of strawberry cream or orange cream."

BARK!

"Stop barking about the biscuits."

"Hey! That's not me," said Jeet.

DING-DONG! The doorbell sounded, followed by a cacophony of barking dogs. A whole pack of dogs, tangled in leads, dribbling oodles of drool, lunged through the doorway with a woman struggling to hold on to them all.

"I'm Tisha and we're from St Saviour's Dog Shelter," shouted the woman over the barking.

Mrs Chandar, Jeet's mum, hurried

forward. She was the local vet and she also helped with the dogs from the shelter. That's how she had become friends with Mrs Barker too.

For the next few minutes, the quiet room turned into an opera of dogs. They barked and whined and lunged from the doorway.

"The dogs are safe," shouted Tisha. "We've just come to pay our respects."

Mrs Chandar led Tisha and the dogs to the mindfulness garden. "Maybe they'd be more comfortable here."

The dogs were let loose in the garden and Tisha found a seat in the front row.

"The dogs will make a mess in the garden," accused Edwin.

But no one paid any attention to his grumbling.

DING-DONG!

The doorbell rang again. A man in a blond wig, dressed in a gold-coloured suit, came into the house.

"King Midas is here," whispered Jeet, still munching on a biscuit.

"My name is Lingam, and I'm Mrs Barker's lawyer," the man announced. "I've come to read Mrs Barker's last will and testament in public as per her wishes."

"This is just like it said in Chapter 7 of my handbook," whispered Sindhu.

"What's going to happen then?" asked Jeet.

"The lawyer will read the will," said Sindhu. "Then if no one objects, he will go away. If someone doesn't agree to the will, it will need to be investigated."

"Fingers crossed," said Jeet. "Let's hope someone disagrees and we get a mystery to solve."

*

The lawyer coughed once. The room quietened and waited in silence. No one made even the tiniest bit of noise until **CRUNCH!** Jeet bit on his orange cream biscuit. The whole room turned and glared at Jeet.

Jeet signed a 'sorry' with his mouth still full of biscuit.

"Thank you for coming," said Mr Lingam, opening a file and pulling out a small sheet of paper. "I'm going to read Mrs Barker's will."

"I leave the house to Edwin, my nephew, even though he doesn't deserve it. I leave my mindfulness garden, a space where I've always been happy in the company of my beloved rescue dogs, to the St Saviour's Dog Shelter."

"What?" screamed Edwin as he rushed to his feet and tried to grab the sheet of paper away from Lingam. "That's not her will. I know she left everything to me, only last month."

"This just got interesting," whispered Sindhu.

"My fingers are still crossed," said Jeet.

"Edwin, this is the latest copy of her will, made on the day she died," said the lawyer. "There was even a witness. Someone called Arjun."

Tisha jumped to her feet. "Thank you to Mrs Barker for this wonderful gift," she said.

Edwin wasn't having any of it. "I hate dogs. I don't want them in my garden."

Mr Lingam shrugged as if he didn't really care.

"Give me that scrap of paper you're

reading from," shouted Edwin, lunging for the lawyer. But Mr Lingam held the will above his head.

Edwin lunged for it again. And this time he grabbed Mr Lingam's wig. There was a ripple of giggles amongst the visitors.

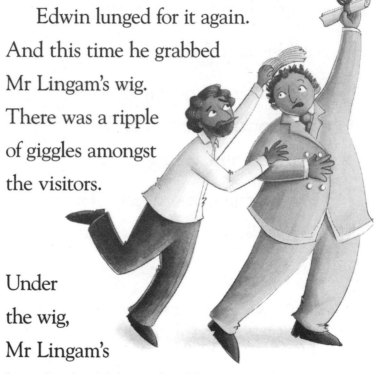

Under the wig, Mr Lingam's hair looked like it had been cut by mice.

"He should get that haircut checked out," said Jeet.

The lawyer hurriedly grabbed the wig off the floor and re-adjusted it on his head. Edwin waved a different sheet of paper in the lawyer's face. "Read this will."

Mr Lingam read the second will and coughed again.

"He should get that cough checked out too," said Sindhu.

"Edwin, the will you have shown me is all good and proper," started Mr Lingam.

Edwin smiled.

"But… it's definitely a week older than the will I read out at first. So, it is now null and void."

"What's that?" he snapped.

"Null and void means it's no longer valid," said Mr Lingam. "Your will is nothing, nada, zilch, zippo, goose egg!"

Edwin was furious. "Look! Can you prove that the new will is actually the latest?" he yelled.

Everyone started whispering simultaneously.

Sindhu winked at Jeet. "Now this gathering is no longer boring. It's a proper mystery," she said.

"And we are going to solve it," said Jeet.

Sindhu got up and shouted. "We're detectives," said Sindhu, "and we've caught fraudsters and burglars."

"Even in London, in England," said Jeet, up on his feet too.

Someone laughed loudly.

Mum stepped forward waving a sheet of paper. "Yes, that's true," she said. "They even have a certificate from their school principal that says they've solved mysteries."

"Mum!" said Sindhu. "You carry that around?"

"I'm proud of you," Mum replied.

"Me too," shouted Mrs Chandar, holding out another copy.

"We better solve the case now," muttered Jeet.

"You know we will," assured Sindhu.

Mr Lingam checked his watch and his phone. "We should really get the police involved," he said. "I can't trust two children with this."

"You can't trust them with biscuits," said Mrs Chandar, with a chuckle. "But you can definitely trust them with the will."

"I want the vet's kid and his friend to solve the mystery," shouted Tisha. "Right here!"

"Me too," said Edwin. "No police, let's get this over with quickly."

*

The visitors, the lawyer, the nephew and the dog lady were all held back by two scary mums turned guards, while Sindhu and Jeet examined the wills.

The old will was typed up on an old-style typewriter and signed by Mrs Barker. Mr Lingam had signed as a witness, on the 22nd of the month.

The other will was handwritten on the back of an old receipt.

"We've to prove that this new will really is in Mrs Barker's handwriting," said Jeet.

"I've an idea," said Sindhu, leading

Jeet to the kitchen. Everyone followed at a respectable distance established by the mums.

Sindhu reached for Mrs Barker's handwritten recipe notebook. It was on exactly the same shelf as her cookbook of dog treats.

"Good thinking," said Jeet.

Sindhu and Jeet compared the handwriting on the scrap will with the notebook.

"It's definitely Mrs Barker's handwriting," said Sindhu.

Tisha smiled for the first time. But Edwin wasn't ready to give up yet.

"Can you prove the new will was

made later than mine?" asked Edwin. "Maybe this dog lady changed the date to a later one."

"That's a good point," whispered Sindhu to Jeet.

Jeet turned to the whiteboard hanging in the kitchen and wrote:

Fact sheet for Mrs Barker's will:

✓ The typewritten will was made on the 22nd.

✓ The handwritten will was made on the 29th.

✓ Mrs Barker died on the 29th.

"Maybe she signed it on the 9th and someone changed it to the 29th?" said Sindhu.

"Miss Tisha, please step forward," said Jeet. "Please write all the Arabic numerals on this whiteboard."

"Why?"

"Don't you know them?" mocked Edwin. "They go from 0 to 9."

Tisha glared at Edwin as she snatched the marker from Jeet's hand and started writing.

Sindhu held her breath as Tisha wrote 0, 1 and 2.

"Nope!" said Jeet. "Her 2 doesn't match the 2 on the paper."

"That's not proof," shouted Edwin. "She's deliberately writing the 2 differently now."

"That's possible," said Sindhu.

Sindhu and Jeet huddled together.

"We've read both these wills, twice," said Jeet. "What are we missing?"

"We only read one side of the paper," said Sindhu, turning over Edwin's typewritten will. The typewritten will had nothing on the other side. But the handwritten will was on the back of a delivery receipt for dog biscuits.

"Look," said Sindhu, jabbing at the last three lines of the receipt.

"Yes!" Jeet cheered and high-fived Sindhu.

*

When Sindhu and Jeet walked into the living room, the room went quiet.

"The will on the delivery receipt was definitely written by Mrs Barker," said Sindhu. "And we can prove it was made later than Edwin's will."

"How?" asked Edwin.

Jeet showed Edwin and Tisha the date and time stamp on the delivery receipt. "Mrs Barker could only have written this will after the dog biscuits were delivered at 4 pm on the 29th."

"Then she decided to change her will," explained Jeet, "so she grabbed the nearest piece of paper, wrote her

will and got someone named Arjun
to witness it."

"I often use the back of delivery
receipts," Mum chimed in. "It's good for
the environment to use both sides of
the paper."

"Well done, you've proved that the
new will is valid," Mr Lingam said. "That
means the house belongs to Edwin and
the garden to the dog shelter."

"But who is Arjun?" asked Edwin.

"The will is valid even if we don't
know who Arjun is. Case closed.
Thank you, Sindhu and Jeet," said
Mr Lingam.

"You're welcome," replied Jeet.

Edwin groaned as Tisha rushed to tell the dogs.

"You did well," said Mum. "I was a bit worried."

"Here, have a biscuit," said Mrs Chandar.

But Sindhu and Jeet weren't listening.

"Are you thinking what I'm thinking?" asked Jeet.

"Who is Arjun?" asked Sindhu.

According to the detective's handbook, all loose ends must be tied up. The mysterious Arjun was a loose end.

DING-DONG!

It was a delivery man with a pack of headphones for Edwin.

Sindhu nudged Jeet. "Look at his badge," she said.

The embossed badge said *Arjun*.

"Let's ask him about it," said Jeet. "I don't like loose ends."

The delivery man confirmed everything they knew. He had indeed signed the will as a witness. Then Mrs Barker had said she was going to order the headphones to be delivered to Edwin too.

"Edwin has a garden full of dogs…" said Sindhu, "and a pair of headphones to block out the noise."

"Mrs Barker had a great sense of humour," said Jeet.

"I'm glad
the dogs got
a place to run
around in," said
Mrs Chandar.

"Thanks to Sindhu and Jeet's
Detective Agency," said Mum, as
she turned on the music and invited
everyone to dance.

"Let's celebrate Mrs Barker's life
just the way she had wanted," said
Mrs Chandar, pulling Sindhu and
Jeet onto the dance floor.

THE MISSING STAR

Sindhu and Jeet were not new to film celebrities. After all, they lived in Kollywood, the nickname for the Tamil cinema industry in Chennai. Their neighbours were actors or directors or lyricists. Most of them were friendly and good-natured.

Ranjith Kumar, the hottest movie star in town, was the friendliest of them all. His last three movies had broken all box office records and he was tipped to win the National Award for Best Actor.

Yet he had no airs and graces. He invited his neighbours for Diwali parties or gave away free tickets to one of his premieres. Fans often waited outside his house to catch a glimpse of him. News cameras camped outside the actor's house night and day. Even Sindhu's dad Mani, a big Ranjith Kumar fan, got annoyed with the crowd once in a while.

One quiet weekend morning, Sindhu and Jeet were watching TV in Jeet's house when the phone rang.

TRING-TRING!

It was Dad. "Ranjith is missing," he said. "Come quickly to his house."

"The actor?" asked Jeet.

"Yes, the actor, how many other Ranjiths do you know?"

"Two," said Jeet, matter-of-factly. "There is one in our quiz team and another in my class."

"Good to know," said Dad. "Come and help me find him. You are detectives, are you not?"

"We're on our way over, Dad," said Sindhu.

Sindhu and Jeet hurried over to Ranjith's house. Outside the tall walls and big iron gates, a big crowd had gathered to catch a glimpse of the actor.

"Psst!"

Dad was waving to them from the service entrance. He led them into the brightly lit living room. Ranjith Kumar's staff stood around with worried looks.

"What's going on, Dad?" asked Sindhu.

"This morning, Ranjith had an appointment with Garuda TV, the most prestigious channel ever. He was supposed to do interviews, a cooking demonstration and play cricket with other stars."

"How do you know this?" asked Jeet.

"He had invited me to come along and play in his cricket team," said Dad.

Sindhu giggled. Dad was a famous photographer in his own right. But he was star-struck when it came to Ranjith Kumar.

"It's not funny, Sindhu," said Dad.

"Uncle Mani," said Jeet, in a reassuring voice. "Why don't you tell us what happened?"

"He asked me to come at 8 am," Dad replied. "It's now after 10 am, and no one can find Ranjith. The TV crew have been calling every ten minutes."

"What have you done so far?" asked Sindhu, pulling out her notebook to write down the clues.

"We've searched every room," said the housekeeper.

"And I've called all his friends," said his personal assistant.

"What time did he leave the house this morning?" asked Jeet.

"We never saw him leave," cried the housekeeper. "He didn't even drink his special coconut water with ginger this morning."

"Maybe that's why he ran away," whispered Jeet. "Who puts spicy ginger into cooling coconut water?"

"Shh," said Sindhu. "Have you called the police?"

The assistant was alarmed.

"No police," he screamed. "Ranjith Sir's reputation will be all over the newspapers. Garuda TV have promised to postpone the event to midday because we told them Ranjith has got the runs."

"The runs?" asked Sindhu. "You don't think that will ruin his reputation?"

"I have three words for you – ginger coconut water," said Jeet, giggling.

But a stern stare from Dad quietened him quickly.

"Any ransom calls?" asked Sindhu.

Everyone shook their heads. "Good," said Jeet. "No ransom calls mean it's not a kidnap."

Dad gasped.

"Mind if we check his bedroom?" asked Sindhu.

The housekeeper took them to the actor's bedroom. Sindhu made observations in her notebook.

Ranjith Kumar is Missing

1	Searched all the rooms – nothing!
2	Called all the friends – no news!
3	Did not go out this morning.

"Nothing seems out of the ordinary here," said Sindhu.

"Over 100 shirts, 24 pairs of jeans," said Jeet. "That is not out of the ordinary for you?"

"Maybe for you," said Sindhu. "Ranjith is a movie star."

They checked the rooms again, looking for hidden spaces behind bookcases or trapdoors to basements. There was nothing suspicious. Then they went into the trophy room. On one side all his trophies and awards were displayed. The other wall was covered with photographs showing Ranjith Kumar in different costumes.

Ranjith as a woman, as a magician, as a street cleaner – he seemed to be a master of disguises.

"I took some of these photos," said Dad. "Way before he became a movie star. We've been good friends ever since. Please, you must find him."

"We will, Dad," said Sindhu. "Try not to worry."

They had looked in every nook and cranny of the house. It did seem that Ranjith Kumar had disappeared into thin air.

*

The house held no more clues. They went to check the garden. The garden had a neatly manicured lawn with flowered borders. The benches were clean and newly painted. The shed was what anyone would expect a shed to look like – full of gardening tools and random stuff. There was no place to hide anyone there.

"Ranjith Sir pays a fortune to the landscapers," said the housekeeper. "More than he pays me."

Was the housekeeper disgruntled? wondered Sindhu. *What if all the staff were involved together?*

"Did you talk to him about it?" asked Jeet.

"Actually, I did," said the housekeeper. "He said he'd take care of it in my Diwali bonus. He's very nice. He even pays for my daughter's school fees."

Sindhu sighed. There went the theory of disgruntled housekeeper.

"What next?" she asked Jeet. "Maybe one of the other staff?"

Jeet interviewed each staff member. They all had been working for Ranjith for over three years.

"Is that everyone?" asked Jeet.

"We've a new gardener," said the housekeeper. "He just started yesterday."

The gardener was old
and wrinkly, with a slight
stoop. He folded his hands
in front of him as he looked
warily at Sindhu and Jeet.

"If Ranjith had an
expensive landscaper," asked
Sindhu, "why did he hire you?"

"To do odd jobs," said
the old gardener with a tremor in
his voice.

Ranjith had called that afternoon
from the cricket club and instructed
the staff to settle the gardener into his
job. The gardener had arrived later in
the evening.

Sindhu and Jeet looked at each other.

"That's so odd to hire a stranger," said Sindhu.

"I'm not a stranger," said the old gardener. "I have known him from when he was a baby."

"You're wasting your time," said Dad to Sindhu and Jeet. "Many famous people hire folks from their native village out of loyalty. Think of something else."

"Let's check the car park," said Sindhu, heading outside with Dad and Jeet following her.

A shiny new car stood next to a shiny new motorbike. The driver explained that the car hadn't been used since the day before, when Ranjith had been dropped off at the cricket club.

Jeet checked the car's boot to make sure no one had locked Ranjith in there. "And the motorbike?" he asked.

"Ranjith Sir takes the motorbike when he wants to go on long drives to be on his own," said the driver.

So Ranjith hadn't driven off into the sunset either. The detectives were stumped. They needed to review the clues.

Sindhu opened her notebook and struck out the word *kidnap* and added the new clues. *Was the answer right in front of them? Why can't we see it?* she wondered.

Ranjith Kumar is Missing

1. Searched all the rooms – nothing!
2. Called all the friends – no news!
3. Did not go out this morning.
4. His clothes are not missing. (Too many clothes!)
5. Suitcases are all here.
6. Cricket kit is still here.

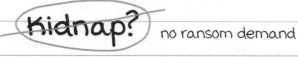 no ransom demand

7. Not hiding anywhere else.
8. Master of disguise.
9. Big garden, managed by landscaper.
10. Is the housekeeper disgruntled? NO!!!
11. Long term staff... except... the old GARDENER!
    He was hired over the phone.
12. Nothing inside the car.
13. The car hasn't been driven at all today.

"The only thing that's bothering me is the gardener," said Jeet. "Maybe he kidnapped Ranjith and has come here to collect the ransom?"

Sindhu nodded.

"Let's talk to the gardener again," she said, hurrying towards the shed.

"Someone's in there," whispered Jeet, pulling Sindhu back, "the door is ajar."

They tiptoed quietly and peeped through the window.

The gardener was texting someone on his phone.

"This man knows how to text?" whispered Jeet.

"Hey! Anyone can learn technology,"

said Sindhu. "Don't judge a person by their age. Maybe he is texting whoever is holding Ranjith."

Jeet gently pushed the door open wider, then he and Sindhu stepped into the shed and shouted in unison. "GOTCHA!"

Startled, the gardener sprang from his seat, and without missing a beat, turned and ran out of the back door.

"This shed has a back door!" shouted Jeet.

"Don't let him escape," yelled Sindhu as they chased the gardener through the vegetable garden at the back. "How come the old man is so quick on his feet?"

"Don't judge
a person by their age," said Jeet.

Sindhu and Jeet were nipping at his
heels when the gardener stomped across
the manicured lawn, jumped over the
newly painted cement bench and hoisted
himself over the wall.

"Go, go!" shouted Jeet to Sindhu.

The gardener turned to glance at
them and jumped over to the other side.

"Give me a boost, Dad!" shouted Sindhu, as Dad and the driver appeared from the front to see what was going on.

Sindhu climbed over the wall with a little boost from Dad. She spotted the gardener in the neighbour's back garden.

Jeet clambered up next. Together they sprinted after the old man out of the neighbour's garden and into the street.

Some people stopped to watch, thinking it was a movie shoot. They cheered for the fugitive gardener.

The old gardener weaved through the crowd and turned a corner. Sindhu and Jeet had almost lost track of him when a motorbike screeched its brakes.

Dad was astride Ranjith's motorbike,
blocking the old man's path.

"Great work, Dad," said Sindhu.

The old man slumped to the ground.

"Let's see if he knows where Ranjith
is," said Dad.

"We've already found Ranjith
Kumar, Uncle Mani," said Jeet.

"Where is he?"

"Right here," said Sindhu.

"Give it up, Ranjith," said Jeet to the old man.

The old man sprang to his feet and patted Dad on the shoulder. "Sorry, Mani, for panicking you. And by the way, no one has ever driven that motorbike except me."

"Desperate times call for cool motorbikes," said Sindhu.

Dad was still staring at Ranjith dressed as a gardener, as if he couldn't believe it.

"Let's go back to the house," said Sindhu, "before a crowd gathers."

The time was quarter to twelve.

The TV crew was due soon.

*

Back in the house, Ranjith took off his wig and make-up.

"A master disguise!" said Dad. "Oh! My parrots! I totally believed it."

"I fooled you all, didn't I?!" said Ranjith Kumar and turned towards the detectives. "Except you two. How did you figure it out?"

"You and the old gardener were never in the same place at the same time," said Sindhu.

"And when we went to question the gardener, he – you – sprinted like Vayu, the god of wind himself," said Jeet.

"Clever kids, eh!" said Dad, proudly. "But I don't understand why. Why did you run away? Is this a new TV show?"

Ranjith Kumar laughed. His familiar good-natured laugh.

"I'm tired – of all the press, the schedules, the interviews, the TV appearances. I couldn't face it one moment longer."

"But that's your job," said Dad.

"My job is acting in a movie," said Ranjith, "but cameras are always in my face even when I'm not on the job. There was no time to be myself, plain old Ranjith from a small village with big dreams."

"What are you going to do now?" asked Sindhu.

"I must tell everyone how I really feel," said Ranjith Kumar. "I hope they understand."

"And?" prompted Jeet.

"Get some me-time!" shouted Ranjith happily.

DING-DONG!

The doorbell rang and the TV crew arrived. They were shocked to see Ranjith Kumar the movie star coming to greet them in sweatpants and flip-flops.

"You're not dressed for the show," the cameraman exclaimed.

"I can explain," said Ranjith Kumar.

And so, in front of the TV cameras, Ranjith announced that he was taking a break from being a celebrity until his mental health improved. "If you're feeling stressed, then talk to someone. I urge you," he told his fans.

When the camera crew left, Dad turned to Ranjith and wished him well.

"Come back soon," said Dad.

"Thank you both," said Ranjith, "for making me face the truth. I hope it'll encourage others, especially my fans, to talk about their anxieties too."

"Won't people bother you on your holiday?" asked Sindhu.

"Ha! I'll think of a new disguise to blend in," said Ranjith.

"I bet we can still find you," said Jeet.

"Cricket, anyone?" asked Dad. "I've an afternoon free, courtesy of Sindhu and Jeet's Detective Agency."

A RING OF MYSTERY

Sindhu and Jeet were at the wedding of Jeet's cousin Mallika. Jeet handed a chart of important aunties to Sindhu. "The most important document of the wedding," he said with a chuckle.

"Where are the uncles?" asked Sindhu.

"The uncles are not as important," said Jeet. "Just call everyone Uncle."

"Is this a different Aunty Kamala?" asked Sindhu, pointing at the picture appearing twice.

THE CHART OF IMPORTANT AUNTIES

Aunty Anu
(Mallika's mum)

Aunty Prema
(Aunty Anu's sister)

Aunty Kamala
(An old family friend/
distant relative)

The groom Vikram's relatives:

Aunty Kamala
(Vikram's dad's
third cousin)

"Nope! She is related to both sides," said Jeet. "Aunty Anu calls her the Family News Channel. She relays the news from both sides of the family."

All the children, including Sindhu and Jeet, were given chores to do. Then it was snack-time in the dining hall. Everyone was joking and laughing and teasing Mallika. This was what Sindhu loved about weddings.

"I hate weddings," said Jeet.

"Why?"

"All the aunties I haven't seen in years keep telling me how cute I was in green nappies when I was a baby!"

Sindhu giggled. "Do you have a photo?"

"You'll never see that photo!"

The main wedding hall was huge. On one end was the stage where the ceremony was going to take place. Rows of chairs were being arranged for the guests. Microphones and speakers were set up for the traditional wedding musicians. A photographer was recording videos and taking still pictures of everything.

That evening, when the groom's family was being settled in, Aunty Kamala made a big fuss about her allocated room. She almost threatened to cancel the wedding if they didn't swap her room from 7 to 18, because 18 was her lucky number.

"Every wedding has a fussy aunt or uncle," whispered Jeet.

"Can I go and say hello to Vikram?" asked Mallika.

"Nope!" said Aunty Anu. "We're not allowed into each other's private rooms. We must meet only in the common area until the wedding is over."

Soon Mallika was whisked away to get ready for one ceremony after another. As expected, Aunty Kamala relayed news back and forth between the families.

*

The next morning, Sindhu and Jeet got ready and met up for breakfast near the dining hall.

"Mallika wants to see you," said one of the aunties. "Hurry! She said it's urgent."

"What's more urgent than breakfast?" asked Jeet.

When they knocked on the door and walked into Mallika's room, it was in disarray. The suitcases were open and the clothes were scattered. Mallika looked like she had been crying.

"What's going on?" asked Jeet. "Are you throwing a tantrum or something?"

"No! Look!" said Mallika and held out her hand, palm down.

"Nice *maruthani*," said Sindhu, looking at the traditional south Indian henna pattern on her fingers.

"Not that," said Mallika. "The emerald ring that Vikram's mother gave me is missing."

"Was it loose?" asked Sindhu. "Did it slip from your finger?"

"No, it was the perfect fit," said Mallika. "I was wearing it last night when we welcomed the groom's family. Then I put it away in its box when I changed for bed."

"Maybe you put it in the wrong box," Jeet suggested.

"I've checked," said Mallika. "Three times."

"Where did you last see it?" asked Sindhu.

"After dinner, I put it away in a carved wooden box and stored it along with my wedding jewellery," replied Mallika. "Everything else was there this morning, except the box with the emerald ring."

"Did you leave the room at all this morning?" asked Sindhu.

"I'm not allowed to leave the room," said Mallika, "but I was in the bathroom for a while, getting ready for the first ceremony. Then I came in here to put on my jewellery and couldn't find the ring."

Mallika explained that the ring

wasn't very expensive but it was Vikram's family heirloom. Nothing else had been taken either.

"Should we tell your mum?" asked Jeet.

"No!" screeched Mallika. "No one should find out. Please find it before the final wedding ceremony. I know you've solved many mysteries in our neighbourhood. Do this for me, please. If anyone finds out the ring is gone, it'll be considered a bad omen and they might stop the wedding."

"Leave it with us," said Jeet. "Sindhu and Jeet's Detective Agency is on the case."

*

When they were alone, Jeet asked, "What do you think?"

"Maybe she did lose it in the muddle of things," said Sindhu. "Because if someone came to steal valuables, they didn't touch any of her necklaces or bangles or earrings."

"I know Mallika," said Jeet. "If she says she didn't lose it and it was taken, then it was taken."

"Then you know what this means, right?" asked Sindhu.

"What?"

"Someone wanted just that ring!" said Sindhu.

"But who?" asked Jeet. "Why?"

"According to *The Handbook for Young Detectives*," said Sindhu, "a culprit needs three things – motive, means and opportunity."

"The motive to steal a family heirloom could be…" Jeet started. "Hmm… Maybe they thought it was an antique?"

"Or to stop the wedding," suggested Sindhu. "For example, to suggest Vikram, the groom, had changed his mind about getting married."

"I don't think it's him," said Jeet. "Even if he wanted to, did he have the opportunity? Remember Aunty Anu said they can't go to each other's rooms."

"So, Vikram couldn't have taken it," said Sindhu. "What if he sent someone to do it for him?"

"No one from the groom's side is allowed into the bride's rooms," said Jeet.

"But…" said Sindhu.

"But what?"

"One person can go to both sides without being told off…"

"Aunty Kamala, with both bride and groom privileges," said Jeet.

"She definitely had the opportunity," said Sindhu. "But what would be her motive?"

But before they could decide their next steps, yet another aunty pulled Jeet's hand.

"Ah, Jeet, you were the cute baby with green nappies," she cooed.

Sindhu giggled. "You've got to show me THAT photo!"

"Keep dreaming," said Jeet.

"Smile!" cried the photographer.

They both turned to give a beaming smile at the camera.

CLICK!

"Photos!" shouted Sindhu.

"Videos," said Jeet.

"Photo Uncle," shouted Jeet at the

retreating back of the photographer,
who was now clicking his camera at
other guests.

The photographer turned around
and barked, "Don't be rude, dude. I'm
not old enough to be your uncle."

"Oops!" said Sindhu.

"Can you show us all the videos and
photos you've taken?" asked Jeet.

Sindhu held her breath, wondering if
he'd refuse.

"There," said the photographer
and pointed at a desk with a computer
on it. "Ask my assistant to show you.
This camera sends over everything
directly to the computer."

"Thank you!" shouted Jeet, walking towards the assistant.

*

Sindhu and Jeet looked at photos taken near the bride's room after dinner. Every aunty from Mallika's family had been inside her room at some point.

"That is Aunty Prema, that's her dad's sister, then that's Mallika's great-aunt, that is of course Aunty Kamala, and her daughter Cousin Grumps…"

"Cousin Grumps is the perfect name for someone with a giant scowl," said Sindhu.

Then there were no photos between 10 pm and 6 am that morning.

"Why is there nothing after 10 pm?"

"Because nothing happens," said the assistant. "We are not CCTV. We're creative wedding photographers."

"CCTV!" cried Jeet.

"Let's check the CCTV," echoed Sindhu.

The main event was about to begin in a quarter of an hour and they had to find the CCTV recordings. As they made their way down to the office, Cousin Grumps bumped into Jeet, literally.

"Hey!" greeted Jeet.

"I hate weddings," Cousin Grumps replied.

"You look pretty," said Sindhu, trying to be nice.

"But apparently not pretty enough," she replied, "to be the bride."

Cousin Grumps floated away to be grumpy somewhere else.

"So, she is jealous of Mallika?" asked Sindhu.

"There were rumours," said Jeet, "that Aunty Kamala had a row with Vikram's parents when the wedding was announced because Cousin Grumps wanted to marry Vikram."

"So Aunty Kamala and her daughter

did have a motive to stop the wedding," said Sindhu.

"Opportunity – tick! Motive – tick!" said Jeet. "Two out of three."

"But did she have the means?" said Sindhu. "Would she have been jealous enough to steal and stop the wedding?"

"Let's find out!"

Sindhu and Jeet hurried across the hall, almost bumping into a lady carrying a tray of coconuts. And then they skidded on water spilt on the floor from a holy ceremony.

*

When they knocked on the office door, a bored manager let them in.

"We need to see the CCTV footage," said Jeet.

"Who are you?" he demanded.

"We're the detectives working on behalf of the bride," said Sindhu.

"Uh? But you're children."

"And detectives," said Sindhu.

"You better show us the CCTV recordings," said Jeet, sounding very officious, "if you don't want the police called and this wedding cancelled."

"Hey, it's the wedding season," said the manager. "If the police turn up here, all my bookings for the month will evaporate like ice cubes on a hot pavement."

"We'll keep it hush-hush," said Jeet.

"If you cooperate," added Sindhu.

"Fine!" the manager said with a sigh. "What do you want to see?"

"Outside the bride's room after 10 pm and until 6 am this morning."

The man tapped on his computer and brought the footage. The video was not as grainy as they had expected.

"Colour HD, latest model," the manager boasted. "So good, right! Weddings are a magnet for thieves. So I invest in the very best state of the art equipment."

"Good for you and us," said Jeet.

They watched the footage closely.

After dinner, a whole group of women came with Mallika to her room. Then one by one everyone left. The door shut and nothing happened for a while.

"Fast forward please," said Jeet.

As the hours went by, the clock on the recording showed 5 am.

Someone dressed in white walked towards the bride's room.

"A ghost," said Sindhu.

The manager chuckled.

"Nope! It's someone from the kitchen bringing the bride her morning coffee."

A few minutes later, a woman in a nightie came towards the door.

She looked this way and that way and gently pushed the door open.

Mallika must not have locked her room after the coffee-deliverer had left.

"Oh, she must have been in the bathroom," said Sindhu, "getting ready for the first ceremony."

The woman in the nightie came out quickly carrying a small box.

"That is Aunty Kamala," said Jeet. "Caught box-handed."

Then Cousin Grumps came into view. She opened the box, looked inside and smiled the most evil grin Sindhu had ever seen.

"Mother and daughter in cahoots," said Sindhu.

"Can we see the groom's side entrance please? Maybe five minutes after this?" asked Sindhu.

The CCTV showed the pair of them going into the room marked 18. The number Aunty Kamala had insisted on because it was a lucky number.

"Thank you, sir," said Jeet. "Please don't utter a word about this to anyone. We'll keep it quiet too. And keep the recording safe please."

"Now what?" said Sindhu, as they

stood outside the manager's door.
"We can't blame them in public," said
Sindhu. "It's almost time for the final
ceremony. If we tell everyone that the
lucky heirloom was stolen, someone will
blame it on bad omens and stop the
wedding. People are superstitious."

"Maybe we can threaten Aunty
Kamala to put the ring back without
anyone noticing," said Jeet.

"I'm not sure she's easily intimidated,
Jeet," said Sindhu. "She'll make a fuss
and stop the wedding on some other
pretext."

"We're stuck between bad omens
and aunty tantrums," said Jeet. "I told
you I hate weddings."

"There is another way," said Sindhu.

"What?"

"Make her hand it over willingly!"

"Keep dreaming."

"Come on, have some faith," said Sindhu. "I have a plan."

Sindhu led Jeet towards the wedding musicians playing at the back of the hall. Vikram was seated on the stage, following the priest's instructions. Aunties and uncles, including Aunty Kamala, were milling about on stage.

Jeet checked the big clock. In a couple of minutes, Mallika would come out in her wedding finery to join Vikram. Jeet hoped Sindhu's plan would work.

Sindhu whispered to the musicians to stop playing their music.

The hall fell silent. Everyone turned around to see what was going on. Mallika's dad hurried down from the stage.

Sindhu tapped the mic. "Hello everyone!" she said loudly.

Mallika's dad was approaching rapidly. He'd grab the mic any minute, Sindhu knew.

"Aunty Kamala has a special surprise for our lovely bride Mallika," said Sindhu, just as Mallika stepped onto the stage.

Everyone clapped. Mallika's dad stopped and turned around to face the stage.

"Aunty Kamala, please present her with the special ring," called Sindhu.

Aunty Kamala's face went from shock to aghast to a frown. Cousin Grumps looked like she was going to explode. As Mallika waited with a smile, Aunty Kamala retrieved the box with the ring from her bag. She put the ring on Mallika's finger with a fake smile. The photographer took a flurry of photos.

Jeet took over from Sindhu. "Mallika was given this ring by Vikram's mum," said Jeet. "Aunty Kamala wanted to present this in public to the bride as a sign of welcome. Who better than the person who bridges our two families?"

Everyone clapped again.

"It's time for the ceremonies to continue," shouted the priest from the stage. "Enough of the sideshow."

Mallika was led away and sat next to Vikram. The musicians resumed their traditional music. The wedding proceeded without any more problems. But Aunty Kamala and Cousin Grumps had disappeared like ice cubes on a hot pavement.

"We saved Mallika's wedding!" said Sindhu.

"And thanks to Sindhu and Jeet's Detective Agency," said Jeet, "thirty more weddings booked at this venue have been saved."

"But there's still one mystery to solve," said Sindhu.

"What's that?"

"Were you really that cute as a baby in green nappies?" said Sindhu. "Show me the photo, please, pretty please!"

"Keep dreaming," said Jeet with a laugh.

READING ZONE!

QUIZ TIME

Can you remember the answers
to these questions?

• At the start of the story, why is
Jeet's enthusiasm inappropriate?

• What clothes does
the lawyer Lingam wear?

• How does Dad help Sindhu and Jeet
catch Ranjith when they're chasing him?

• Who is on the Chart of Important
Aunties twice? Why?

READING ZONE!

WHAT DO YOU THINK?

In the second story, Ranjith tries to run away when he realises Jeet and Sindhu have found him. In the end, Ranjith is grateful to them for getting him to face his worries.

Why do you think Ranjith found it difficult to face his worries?

Have you ever felt anxious about something and not been able to tell anyone?

READING ZONE!

STORYTELLING TOOLKIT

This book has three different mystery stories in it. Each one involves people Jeet and Sindhu know.

Which character did you like the most? Why?

Were there any characters you did not like?

How did the author show that they aren't good people?

READING ZONE!

GET CREATIVE

Imagine you are a writer. Can you design a mystery to write about?

Make some notes about what the mystery is, what clues there are and how the characters solve it. You could then write up your own mystery story.